BROKEN PROMISES

About the author

From a very young age, I have had a deep passion for reading books and writing short stories. Writing for me is very therapeutic and is a way for me to express my feelings. It helps me to unload the millions of thoughts that go through my head on a daily basis. I include things about myself in my books, like my thoughts, because I feel like t makes it have a part of me and a sense of belonging.

Aizah Aziz

BROKEN PROMISES

Vanguard Press

A CIP catalogue record for this title is
available from the British Library.

ISBN 978 1 784655 02 0

*Vanguard Press is an imprint of
Pegasus Elliot MacKenzie Publishers Ltd.*
www.pegasuspublishers.com

First Published in 2018

**Vanguard Press
Sheraton House Castle Park
Cambridge England**

Printed & Bound in Great Britain

Acknowledgments

I would like to say a massive thank you to all at Pegasus publishers for giving me the opportunity of a lifetime and helping me make my biggest dream a reality. I would also like to thank my parents and all of my family and friends who have been so supportive of me and this journey of mine. Your support and love means the world to me.

Dedication

To my best friend, Anam.

This one is for you. You always support me when it comes to my writing and just in general. You bought me a notebook which I first wrote this book in and then I visited you in hospital and I told you that I would finish this book for you and get it to you as soon as I could. You were my motivation while I wrote this book and I wanted to keep my word and finish it for you. Thank you for giving me the push I needed. This one's yours.

Love you always,

Aizah.

x

Chapter One

"You ready, Hol? It's nearly time," Susan Callington asked her daughter once she finished getting her ready.

"As ready as I'll ever be. I'm so anxious though," A very nervous Holly Callington replied as she stood in front of the mirror in her hotel room, smoothing out her dress multiple times, making sure that there were no creases.

She studied herself in the mirror. She stood in a white lace wedding dress that hugged her slim figure in all the right places, her train neatly spread on the floor. Her hair was tied up in a loose bun. A few loose, brown curls accompanied her fringe at either side of her face, helping frame her face. She couldn't help but think that there was something missing but she didn't know what. She had her dress on, her hair done, her make-up done (it was subtle the way she liked it), her earrings and necklace were on and, of course, she had her heels on.

"You look beautiful, darling, stop worrying." Her mother reassured, standing behind Holly with her hands on Holly's shoulders.

"Are you sure?"

"Yeah. I do have something for you though," she rummaged around in her bag and pulled out a small black box. "This was your grandmother's. She wanted me to give it to you on your wedding day," Susan continued as she handed Holly the box.

Before she opened it, Holly started to well up at the thought of her late grandmother and how sweet it was of her to leave something for her. She opened the box and inside was a stunning, delicate, silver bracelet.

"Oh my god, Mom. It's beautiful," she exclaimed, her voice breaking. "Can you put it on me?"

"Of course, sweetheart. Now less of the tearing up, you don't want to ruin your make-up!" her mother said as she put the bracelet on her daughter and turned her around so she could see herself in the mirror. They both looked in the mirror and a moment of silence passed between them.

"It just completes the look. I knew there was something missing! Don't you think?" Holly asked, looking at her mother in the mirror to which she smiled and nodded. "I just wish she was here," Holly continued as she looked down at her bracelet and ran her fingers over it.

"I know, me too. She would have been so proud of you, just like I am." Susan beamed with pride as she took one last look at her daughter before they left.

There he was. The man of her dreams. Her best friend. Her everything – Brad Allan. He stood at the altar, dressed smart in his crisp, black tuxedo. It was tailored to perfection, highlighting his tall, slim frame. He looked so perfect and she honestly couldn't believe, even after four years of dating, that he was hers. She walked slowly down the aisle as she held onto her father's arm, hoping that she wouldn't trip. She reached where Brad was standing and her father gave her a kiss before leaving them to get on with it. Brad looked at her and had the biggest grin on his face. He felt so lucky in that moment, to be standing next to her. She mimicked the smile on his face as she looked into his hazel eyes. Everything was just perfect, from his neat comb over to the flower archway and blush rose petals scattered on the floor. It was everything she had ever dreamt of. They said their vows and for the rest of the day, they both wore the biggest smiles and enjoyed their big day.

Once the wedding was over, the happy couple made it to their hotel room, both completely exhausted. Brad sat on the bed and let out a big sigh of relief before he undone his bow tie and rolled up his sleeves. Holly sat at the edge of the bed and began taking her hair pins out, her hair falling out forming perfect loose curls. She turned around and smiled at the sight of her sleepy husband. Clearly the day was too much for him. They sat in silence for a few minutes, both deep in thought reflecting on their day.

"I don't know about you but I am tired!" Brad broke the silence between them, joining her at the foot of the bed.

"That makes two of us! I just want to sleep," Holly replied, taking a break from her hair.

"You looked beautiful today," he said and took a moment to admire her. Even with her hair half out, he still thought that she looked gorgeous.

"Thank you. Did you have a good day today?"

"I did. It was perfect. The set up and everything was exactly the way we asked for which was good because it cost a lot of money!"

Holly laughed at this comment. He was such a successful lawyer so he had plenty of money but he was so picky with what he spent it on. Not to mention that he was extremely fussy and paid great attention to detail when it came to wedding planning. He was probably more stressed out with the planning than she was and kind of took over but she didn't mind because it meant that there was less for her to do.

"Can I promise you something?" he asked, putting his arm around her.

"Sure, go ahead," she replied as she placed her head on his shoulder.

"I promise you, that I'm going to look after you and always give you everything you deserve. OK?"

"Aww, Brad! That's so sweet. Thank you. I will do the same for you."

He smiled. "That's my girl. Now hurry up with that." He pointed to her hair before continuing, "We have an early flight tomorrow and we are not missing it!"

Chapter Two

The sun peered through the curtains and the sound of the waves of the ocean softly hitting the shore, filled her ears. Through the slight gap in the curtain, she could see the crystal blue waters and the white sand that surrounded the crowds of tall palm trees. It was honestly like a dream, so surreal and incredible in every way. She heard a rustle coming from next to her which disrupted her from taking in the beauty of the Maldives. She turned her attention to Brad who was finally wakening up, letting out a few loud yawns.

"Morning!" Holly chirped, sitting up so she was leaning against the headboard and she gazed lovingly at her husband.

"Mornin'," he mumbled in response.

He was really not a morning person whereas she was. They were opposites in a lot of ways but maybe that's why they were attracted to each other and got on so well, opposites did attract after all.

"Look at the view Brad!" Holly exclaimed as she opened up the curtains and let out a small squeal.

To say she was excited about being there would have been an understatement. She had been looking forward to going away for so long and she was so glad that she was finally out of Los Angeles. She did love it in L.A. but she just needed a break from it all. It was

Brad's turn to sit up now, accepting the fact that he wasn't going to get any more sleep, unfortunately for him.

"It's quite spectacular isn't it?" he replied. He admired the view himself and felt rather proud that all of his planning and good choice had paid off.

"It is! I am so excited to go out and explore," she said. She felt like a child again, so full of joy and excitement.

***

Later that day, they had decided to go out for an early dinner at one of the close by Italian restaurants. It was just what they needed after a long afternoon of exploring. The receptionist at their hotel had recommended a restaurant and mentioned that it was quite a fancy place so they had decided it was best to make an effort. Brad looked handsome in a white shirt, jeans and a pair of loafers. His brown hair was in its usual comb over style, not one hair out of place. She wished he would leave his hair natural without any product in it but he never listened to her, not when it came to his hair. They sat at their table as they waited for their meals to be served. Mellow music played softly in the background which suited the place so well. It was a beautiful restaurant that overlooked the water; it filled her with warmth and gave her a fuzzy feeling inside. The cheerfulness of the waiters and waitresses contributed to the lovely atmosphere of the restaurant.

"I cannot wait to eat!" a hungry Brad said as he adjusted the watch on his wrist.

"Me neither," Holly agreed, glancing over to the kitchen to see if there was any sign of their food coming. "You know, this is really nice," she continued. "It's nice to spend some time together. I feel like before the wedding we were both so busy and stressed, you a little more than me, and we were just so wrapped up in it all."

"Yeah, that's true. I'm so glad that's all over and done with. I just wish I could forget about work now and really unwind. It's going to be so hectic when I go back, so it's actually good that we are spending this time together here."

"Ugh, don't talk about work," she groaned. "I'm not looking forward to going back either. It's not even bad, the job. I like being an accountant but I'm just used to being off the last few weeks and I just want to live in this little happy bubble with you forever."

"I hate to burst your bubble but we will be getting back to reality soon, sunshine."

"I know, I know."

"Hey, cheer up. We still have a good couple of days left here! And look, your food's coming." He nodded towards the waiter who was approaching their table, his hands full with three plates of food.

Her eyes lit up at once. Whoever said *'The way to a man's heart is through his stomach.'* clearly didn't know her because the way to her heart was through her stomach. She was a foodie for sure and she was always happy when there was food involved, there was no denying that. She said her thanks to the waiter and began digging into her food.

"Wow. This is good," she said when she finished her first couple of bites. She was definitely impressed by the quality of the food.

"I think you were even hungrier than I was, gosh." he replied before he began to eat his own food.

Once they finished their meals, they headed outside for a walk along the beach before they went back to their hotel. They made it out just in time to witness the most perfect sunset. The pink sky could be seen in the reflection of the slow-moving water next to them. Grains of sand could be felt between her toes as she walked hand in hand with Brad. A group of boys could be seen in the near distance, passing a ball back and forth between them. They looked so free and relaxed, not a care in the world, although there were a few shouts that came from them but that was just boys being boys. As they approached the group, the ball rolled in their direction and Brad stopped it with his foot. One of the boys came forward to retrieve the ball. He looked like he was in late teens, early twenties, just like rest of his group.

"She's hot," one of the other boys mumbled to another, loud enough for both her and Brad to hear. Holly rolled her eyes and shrugged it off as she waited for Brad to give the ball back so they could go.

"What did you just say?" Brad snapped, the anger clear in his tone. He picked up the ball and tucked it under his arm, no intention of giving it back.

"Leave it, Brad. Just give the ball back and let's go," Holly pleaded.

"You heard her," the boy spoke, walking towards Brad with his hands out for the ball.

"You better apologise for being so disrespectful."

"Oh yeah, or what?"

"Trust me, you don't want to know," Brad said, the anger was building up inside of him and his hand curled into a fist.

"Brad, let's go," Holly pleaded again. She took the ball from Brad and threw it back to the boy.

The rest of their walk home was quiet, nothing but silence between them. She was so annoyed about the way that he had acted.

"Brad," Holly spoke, wanting to address the earlier situation.

"What Holly? What is it?" Brad snapped back. He was still clearly in a mood.

"What did I tell you about flying off the handle like that? They were only kids, jeez."

"Well that doesn't mean that they have the right to be disrespectful."

"You said you'd calm down with all that. All you had to do was ignore it and walk away. You're thirty years old!!"

"I have been calm! It's been months since I've been angry about anything. Is that not good enough for you, huh? And you, by the way, didn't exactly help matters there, treating me like a child."

"You would have ended up punching the boy or something if I hadn't stepped in. But you're right, I'm sorry. You actually haven't snapped in a while. I just hate it when you get angry like that."

"I know, I'm sorry too. I should have remained calm. I promise it won't happen again. OK?" Brad reassured, giving her a smile.

"OK, thank you," she said as they embraced each other in a quick hug.

Chapter Three

She sat on the sofa, a cup of hot chocolate in her hand, watching T.V. or at least trying to. She just couldn't concentrate and she knew exactly why. It was seven-thirty p.m. and she was still waiting for Brad to get home from work. She wasn't quite sure where he was. He was usually home for six-thirty p.m. so he was an hour late and he wasn't answering his cell. That left her with only one thing to do – worry. Of course she was going to worry. He usually did mention something if he was going to be late but that morning before they both left to go to work, he never said anything about coming home late. She got up and paced back and forth in the living room, the worst thoughts flowing through her mind. She even tried calling his friend and co-worker and he had said that Brad had left work on time so surely he should have been home by now.

"Maybe he just went to the store after work or something," she thought to herself, calming down with the pacing. She decided that she needed to calm down a little and not assume the worst. She would give it another ten minutes before she went out and looked for him herself. She didn't know if that would even help the situation but it would help her sanity.

She sat back down and tried to tune back into the programme that she had put on earlier.

Once the ten minutes had passed, she picked up her phone and thought that she would try and call him one last time, maybe now he would answer. Just as she was about to call, the doorbell rang and she sprung out of her seat, hoping that it would be him. A look of relief could be seen on her face when it was indeed Brad who stood there at the other side of the door. She threw her arms around him at once and let out a big sigh.

"Good evening, Holly. You OK?" Brad asked after returning her hug, a little puzzled.

"Where the heck have you been? You're so late. I've been trying to call you for ages!" Holly shouted as she let him into the house.

"Oh yeah, my battery died. Sorry. I just had some things to do after work."

"You could have mentioned that. I've been so worried about you. I thought something had happened."

"I'm fine, Holly."

"I even called Sam and he didn't know where you were either."

"Woah, what are you like keeping tabs on me or something? You didn't need to worry. I don't need to tell you everything, you know. Start worrying if I go missing for a few days, not hours," he snapped, a scowl forming on his face.

"Maybe I won't even bother worrying at all next time," she muttered under her breath, unaware that he had heard her.

"What was that?" he asked, putting a hand behind his ear as if to try and hear her clearer even though he didn't need to.

"Nothing."

"What was that?" he repeated and gripped her arm tightly.

"Ouch, you're hurting me. Let go!" She gasped and struggled with him to get away. Only he didn't and instead gripped her arm even tighter.

"Are you going to lose the attitude?" he asked, raising his eyebrows.

"Yeah. I'm sorry," she said.

He let go and she let out a cry and rubbed her arm where it hurt, the marks of where his fingers dug into her skin clearly visible.

"I'm so sorry," he apologised, running his finger over the marks on her arm. "I promise that won't happen again. OK?"

She nodded. She knew it was all her fault and that she deserved it. She shouldn't have had attitude but she couldn't help the fact that a tear still rolled down her cheek as she glimpsed at her arm.

"Don't cry, it makes you look like a child. It's not that sore, is it?" he asked.

"No, you're right. I'm sorry. It's nothing," she confirmed, giving him a faint smile.

"Good. Now let's enjoy the rest of the evening huh?"

"Yeah," she replied, wiping the tear from her face.

***

A few days had passed since the incident and Holly was so glad that it hadn't happened again. In fact, it was like nothing had even happened. They were both happy and he hadn't snapped again since then. He was treating her to a shopping trip and he seemed to be fine so she had no fears about anything happening again. He promised her and she was sure that he would keep it. She was actually excited to have a day out with him; he had been working late recently so they never had a chance to do much. She wandered around the store, near the fitting room as she waited for Brad to finish trying on his clothes. She couldn't really be bothered trying anything on herself, she was quite lazy when it came to that.

"Holly?" Brad called from inside the fitting room.

"Yeah? Just coming," she replied and hurried back to where he was. He was trying on a new suit for his work party and she had to admit, he looked very nice. The navy D&G suit fitted him perfectly, not too tight and not too loose.

"What do you think? It looks good, right?" he asked, admiring himself in the mirror.

"Check you out. I love it! I think you should get it, for sure!"

"Yeah, I am going to. I already decided. I just thought that I better ask you before you go moody." They both chuckled at his comment.

"Good. You're learning," she said, a smile appearing on her face.

"Right, let me just get out of this and we will go to that cafe across the street. How does that sound?" he suggested.

"Perfect, I could do with a snack."

Later at the cafe, they both indulged in a slice of cake each. It was a cool place with lots of bright colours and crazy patterns on the walls. It was quite a quiet place but it still had a nice atmosphere nonetheless. A few bites into his cake, Brad stopped and put down his spoon. He looked nervous and as though he had something on his mind. He did, he had been thinking about something for a while and had been meaning to ask Holly for a few days but he wasn't sure how she would take it. She noticed the worried expression on his face and became curious.

"You OK? Is it not nice?" Holly asked, her eyebrows raised as she waited for a response.

"Uh yeah, very nice. I actually need to ask you something," he said with a serious look on his face.

"Oh OK, what's up?"

"I've been thinking, how nice would it be to move to Morro Bay?" he exclaimed.

"You what? Why? This is both of our hometowns. I've always stayed here."

"Exactly. Are you not fed up of being in the same place this whole time? Not to mention, there's so many nosy people here in Beverly Hills."

"That's true. What about work though?" she asked, wondering if it would work.

"Oh, we have an office there too." he reassured. "You could just get another job. And we will be nearer the seaside so that will be nice, huh?"

"Are you serious about this?" she quizzed, now putting her own spoon down and really thinking about his offer.

"Yes! Don't you wish you could just start afresh sometimes?"

"I do. Ah, it's so tempting!"

"Come on! It will be good for us," he pleaded, giving her hand a light squeeze.

"You know what, I'm in! I can always come back and visit the family and friends, I guess."

"Of course. We will definitely come back when we have time."

"OK, let's do it! Oh my god. I can't believe we are actually going to move," she squealed, getting excited after coming around to the idea. Not that it took her much persuading.

"Great. I'll call and sort out the house I picked!" He said as he pulled out his phone not wanting to waste any time.

Chapter Four

The huge house was located at the seaside with an incredible view of the water and small strip of golden sand. It was fabulous. It was a four bedroom which they really didn't need but Brad insisted that it was the house for them. At least if they were to have kids in the future, they wouldn't have to move. The house featured a spacious kitchen that had black cupboards and drawers, white marble worktops and her favourite part – an island in the middle which contained some drawers and cupboards around it. The white tiles that covered the floor were the perfect finish. The whole place was amazing, like one of those houses you saw on Instagram. Their bedroom and bathroom, however, were her favourite places in the whole house. They were both pastel colours, lots of blush and cream and it just made her happy. When she got a job, it would be the perfect place to come to when she got home after a long day.

It was their second day in their new house and it was going to be just as long as their first one, considering how much unpacking they had to do. It was going to take ages to get everything unpacked and for them to settle in. Just as well she wasn't working at the moment. The clock had just struck ten a.m. so she sprung out of bed to get ready for her long day ahead. The sooner she started, the sooner she could be done for the day. Luckily, she had Brad's help today too as he had the day off but it wouldn't be until later as he loved a lie in when he was off and she didn't want to disturb him so she just got on with it. After what felt like ten hours had passed (it was only three), Brad came down the stairs finally ready to help with the unpacking. Holly was too busy in a day dream to even notice that he was in the kitchen with her. He cleared his throat when he realised that she was unaware of his presence.

"Oh, hey! Sorry I never saw you there," Holly said when she realised he was there.

"Afternoon. What were you busy thinking about?" he asked.

"Nothing."

He raised an eyebrow in response to her answer. "It was obviously something, tell me."

"It's really nothing but OK. I was just thinking about work. A little bit stressed that I've not got a job and I don't know how long it will take me to get one," she admitted with a glum look on her face.

"Ah, I see," he responded. "Well, you shouldn't stress. You don't even need a job."

"Uh, yeah I do."

"No, you don't. I'm serious. I obviously earn more money and I can afford to provide for both of us. So you don't actually need a job. What do you think?"

"No," she spoke, shaking her head in disapproval.

"No?" he repeated, his tone becoming firm. He slowly walked towards her.

"I mean, I'll think about it."

"Good. It would just mean you will be around more to do things in the house and you won't have silly paperwork that you always do when you get home from work so we could spend that extra time together."

"Hmm…"

"Have a think, Holly," he said as he patted her shoulder.

He knew that it would be the best thing to have her at home where he would have all of her attention. You see, he didn't really like the idea of her going out without him, unless it was very important and her job was hardly that important. It was just silly accounts where she would probably never even progress so it was pointless. Now, if she took up his offer to stay at home, her mind wouldn't be so preoccupied with work. It would just make his life so much easier and hers, of course. It would work for both of them.

Later that day, she was still thinking about Brad's offer as she began to put the dishes in their correct cupboards. It would be amazing for her to not work and not have that stress but she didn't want to have to be fully dependent on him all the time. Another thing that crossed her mind was how bored she would be stuck in the house. She looked over at Brad who was across the island in the kitchen, putting the glasses away in the cupboard. She was so in love with him but she wasn't sure if she could give up work for him. It was a big thing, a thing she wasn't quite ready for.

"How you getting on there?" she called over to Brad.

"Not bad, this box is almost done and then I think that's all of our mugs and glasses sorted so that's good," he replied, continuing with what he was doing.

"Ah, that's good! We're getting there, slowly but surely."

"Yes. So, have you given my offer any further thought?" he asked the dreaded question as he turned his attention towards her.

"Yeah about that… I think I'm gonna decline your offer. As lovely as it is, I just can't not work. I've always worked for as long as I can remember and I can't imagine just sitting at home all the time. I'd go crazy."

"Oh. Here's me thinking you would actually want to be home more and want to spend more time together without the stress of work bothering you," he said.

A look of disappointment mixed with sadness appeared on his face and she instantly felt a pang of regret. Maybe she should have just gone along with it.

"Are you sure you have thought this through properly? I'm giving you the opportunity of a lifetime," he continued.

"Yeah, I'm sorry. Thank you though."

"Are you sure?" He repeated, his tone much more firm this time as he took a few steps towards her. Her heart started racing as she had flashbacks of the last time she was foolish and he had got angry.

"Uh, you know what. Maybe it's not such a bad idea after all. You're my number one priority so if you want me to stay home, then that's what I will do," she spoke softly.

"Good. It will be better for you this way. I thought you were going to stick with your silly decision for a second."

She gulped, "Of course not." She gave him a weak smile and continued to unpack the box of dishes.

He smiled. This was really good for him. He loved to be in control and this was him getting there. He would be who she depended on. He would be in control when it came to finances because her money would run out soon. He already had some control over her. He had moved her here and she was willing to do anything for him. She even left her family and friends for him, which was his plan all along because there would be no one in their new area to interfere and no one she could go running to. She knew how he felt about her going back to Beverly Hills without him. He made it seem like he would be deeply hurt if he didn't get to go and see the family, when in fact, he couldn't care less. He wasn't much of a family person. The icing on the cake now was that there was no work to worry about, no one could find out anything about him or them so it was great. Everything was going just the way he had planned.

Chapter Five

She pulled back the duvet and dusted her bedding, getting ready to climb into bed and sleep. Brad stood on the other side of the bed, taking off his cufflinks and undoing his tie. Just as she was about to get into bed, she saw the pile of ironed clothes on the chair from the corner of her eye and thought that she would just quickly put them away. She began putting them away and Brad got into bed, his eyes looking tired. He was tired after the day he had at work and all he wanted to do was sleep but she still had the light on so that wasn't happening.

"Oh, Holly. I meant to say, I'm going out after work tomorrow so don't wait up," he said, running his fingers through his hair.

"Again?" she asked. She was getting tired of his new routine of going out pretty much every day.

"Yes. Is that a problem?" he replied, rolling his eyes.

"You've been going out a lot recently, that's all."

"And? I work hard so I deserve some time to chill."

"Yeah but you could just chill at home. You better not make this a habit."

"Excuse me? Who do you think you are?" he hissed.

"Just ignore me, sorry," she said quickly, hoping that the situation wouldn't escalate.

"I don't think so," he spat, jumping out of the bed and making his way towards her, full of rage.

She really wished, in that moment, that she had just kept her mouth shut. She knew exactly what was about to happen. He came closer to her and once he was close enough, he pushed her into her dressing table and grabbed her face.

"Say that now," he snapped and a smirk formed on his face.

She winced, unable to get any words out. He was superior in that moment, his six-foot frame was already towering over her five foot three one but he was superior in other ways. He had control over her and made her feel like a silly little girl. He glared at her with his eyes wide and a disgusted look on his face.

"I'm sorry," she mumbled. Her whole body was shaking beneath his touch and she just about got the words out with her face being squashed.

"What was that?" he asked, twisting her arm with his free hand as he spoke.

"I'm sorry," she repeated, trying to sound as clear as she could.

"Good girl. You went too far, you know that," he spoke. His anger was calming down as he slowly released her from his grip. She nodded her head vigorously in response to his statement. "Get up, let's go to sleep." he finished.

Chapter Six

One year later

It was twelve p.m. on a sunny Monday afternoon and Holly had decided to venture out and explore one of the nearby towns while Brad was at work. She took off her wedding ring and placed it carefully in her bag because she couldn't be bothered with any questions or anything that indicated to her being married. She was dressed casually in a pair of jeans, a t-shirt and sneakers. She was just going for a walk so she didn't really care what she looked like.

The street she walked through was a cobbled one on a slight hill. It was the cutest place ever, surrounded by small stores and houses. There were a few busy cafes in close view that had inside and outside seating which evidently came in handy considering there were not many spare seats outside. The sunshine definitely helped with that. She made her way through the street, occasionally going into a store and chatting to the locals to ask what the area was like or if they had any recommendations. It had been a year since she had moved to Morro Bay and she really liked it. It was very different to Beverly Hills but a good different. There was none of that hustle and bustle or typical L.A. traffic but instead, there was a lot of peacefulness and quietness. An elderly couple sat outside one of the cafes, talking and laughing. The man fed his wife some of his cake and just the sight of them being so adorable was enough to make her head towards that cafe, called Tyler's. It looked like a cosy cafe and she needed a break from all of the walking she had done so she went in, the elderly couple gave her warm smiles as she passed them which she returned.

She walked in and it was indeed cozy. It was a neutral place, cream and a really pale mint green. There were sofas with cushions and, of course, a table, in certain areas whereas other areas had standard table and chairs. A wide variety of cakes and biscuits were displayed beneath the counter, all looking very tempting. She stood at the counter and that's when she saw him. A tanned young man stood opposite her, a little busy doing something on the cash register to even realise she was there. It just meant she could get away with staring at him for a while longer. He had brown tousled hair with the sides slightly shaved. He looked up finally and she quickly diverted her eyes to the menu lying on the counter.

"Oh, I'm so sorry. I didn't realise you were standing there," the tall and trim man spoke, his voice soft. "What can I get for you?"

"That's OK," she said, giving the guy a smile which he returned. "Can I get a caramel latte please?"

"Of course. Sit in or take-away?"

"Sit in please."

"OK, anything else?"

"No, that's all thanks."

"That's $2.50 please." he said, hitting a few buttons on the cash register. "Thanks, just take a seat and I'll have someone bring it over as soon as it's ready," he continued once she gave him the money.

"Thanks," she said.

"I'm Tyler by the way, Tyler Hawkins," he blurted, smiling again. A small crease formed at either side of his eyes.

"Nice to meet you, Tyler," she replied and gave him another smile.

"You new here?"

"Yeah, kind of." She finished the conversation with that and made her way to find a seat.

It was a busy cafe. There were some chairs sticking out after people clearly refused to tuck them in once they were finished so she dodged her way through them and finally found an empty seat. She sat down and studied Tyler properly, without making it obvious. He was busy serving more customers and she couldn't help but watch and get lost in his beauty. He had the prettiest blue eyes she had ever seen and a perfectly chiselled jaw line that could still be made out through his light beard. If she wasn't married, she would have definitely got his number. Of course, she felt bad for brushing him off and being blunt with him but she couldn't give anything away, not when her husband was a bit crazy. He had told her that he didn't want her to go out without him so she had to sneak out while he was at work and make sure she was back in time so that he would never know.

Tyler stood behind the counter mesmerised by a pretty brunette girl who was sitting, sipping her latte. He couldn't take his eyes off her. She was exactly what he looked for in a girl – looks wise – and she seemed nice too so that was good. She was a little dry with him but they did only just meet so that was fair enough. He wanted to know more about her but he was indecisive about whether to go over or not. He didn't want to come across weird and too eager to her but at the same time he didn't want to miss his chance, he had no idea if he would ever see her again.

***

That evening, she left Brad downstairs as he was happily watching the news and made a start on her ironing. There was a bundle of clothes that were accumulating in the laundry room and she had been putting it off for a few days. Her mother would have scolded her if she had seen how lazy she had been. She grabbed Brad's shirt from the pile of clothes and placed it on the ironing board. She attempted to iron it and felt the shirt stick to the iron and immediately started to panic. *"No, no, no, no, no, please don't be burnt,"* she thought to herself, quickly lifting the iron up. She plucked up the courage to take a look at the shirt and of course, it was burnt. It was just her luck.

"Ugh!" she groaned in frustration.

She usually always checked the iron and the settings before she used it but the one time she didn't, it ended up in a disaster. It had to be his shirt as well.

It just had to be. If it was anything of hers, she wouldn't care as much but it was his and it was designer. He was going to be mad, real mad. Maybe if she threw it out, he wouldn't notice it was missing and everything would be fine. At least that's what she was hoping for. Just as the optimistic thought left her mind, Brad ran up the stairs with a curious look on his face as he wondered what had happened.

"You OK?" He asked after opening the door to the laundry room. He leaned against the door frame as he waited for a response.

"Yeah." She gulped.

"Oh, I heard someth —." He stopped mid-sentence when he saw the shirt and a look of anger appeared on his face. "Is that my shirt?" he said quietly, the anger clear in his voice and on his face.

"I'm so sorry. It was an accident. Please don't freak out," she pleaded, her breathing getting faster and faster.

"Do you know how much that cost me? It's designer!"

"I'm sorry. I'll buy you another one."

He stormed into the room with his blood boiling and grabbed the iron that was switched off but still hot. She let out a gasp as he held it up and gripped her wrist.

"Brad, please don't. I will do anything to make it up to you, I promise. Just please don't hurt me," she begged as she began to well up.

Her words didn't seem to register in his head. All he could see was red and there was no getting through to him. He held the iron so that the pointed part was facing her and placed it on her skin for a few seconds, making sure he kept hold of her arm so she couldn't get away.

"AHHHHH!" she screamed out in pain, desperately trying to free herself.

After a few seconds, he put the iron back on the board and let out a sigh. "You pathetic little girl. You know for a twenty-five-year-old, you're pretty stupid," he snarled and left her sobbing, closing the door behind him.

She ran to the bathroom at once and put her arm under the cold water. It was so painful for a small burn. The tears kept flowing from her eyes and she was full of hatred for him. She didn't know who he was anymore; it sure wasn't the man that she fell in love with. That was the last straw for her though. That was it. She wanted a divorce as soon as possible. She wanted out.

Chapter Seven

She stuck her two fingers down her throat until she started to gag and all of her breakfast came out. That's what her marriage was doing to her, making her ill. Two weeks ago, Brad had made fun of how she looked in a top she was wearing and called her fat then told her that she needed to go to the gym more often. She felt so humiliated and her making herself sick is what it had led to. That was the thing with certain people, they would say what they wanted to then later, they would say that they didn't mean it or that it was just a joke but little did they know that the receiving person would cling to those words and never forget them. It was only a fairly new thing that she had started doing but she could already feel herself becoming addicted to it. She couldn't imagine having a meal and actually keeping it down. All she craved was the satisfaction that she got afterwards. That feeling that she was in control over what stayed in her body was everything to her and all she cared about. She revelled in the fact that it was working and she was losing weight but she had no idea how much the whole thing was about to consume her.

She retched and retched until no more food was coming out and she got up off of the bathroom floor. She wiped the tears that had fallen – she wasn't really sure why they came out – and she rubbed her knuckles so that they wouldn't look so red and to Brad, it would look like nothing had ever happened. He didn't know that she was making herself sick. She tried to do it mostly when he was at work or when he was busy at home, which was often. She knew that he probably wouldn't care but she just wanted to keep it to herself.

Things weren't great between them. She was so fed up with him and all of his anger issues. She had tried to get a divorce but all he did was laugh in her face and refuse to sign the papers. She thought about telling someone, like the police or her parents but she came to the conclusion that it wouldn't work. The police would need evidence and she never had any. Her mom got ill when she was stressed and Holly didn't want to put her mother through that and her father, well he loved Brad. Brad had reminded her of all of these facts when she had threatened him that she would tell and she believed him. He had managed to convince her that no one loved her and no one would believe her. He had told her that he couldn't lose her and so she had to stay in the marriage, if you could even call it that. They hardly went out and just argued so often which led to him beating her. It was horrible for her but she just had to get on with it.

Chapter Eight

"Here you go, new girl!" Tyler said, putting down a caramel latte on the table for Holly who sat in the same seat as the last time she was in the cafe.

He was still mesmerised by her beauty. She wore her hair down in loose waves, was dressed in a checked shirt and jeans and had minimal make-up on. So simple, yet so beautiful.

"Thank you," she thanked him with a smile and continued to read the book that she was reading.

"So, what's your story?" he asked, sitting on the chair across from her with an intrigued look on his face.

"My story? I don't have one."

"Oh, come on. Everyone has a story."

"OK, but you're a stranger so why would I tell you my story? And just out of curiosity, do you talk to all new people like this?" she asked, placing her book down to give him all of her attention.

He was sat observing her as she observed him. He too, was dressed casually in a pair of jeans and plain black t-shirt. Something that Brad would never wear or suit but Tyler pulled it off so well. His hair was hidden under a baseball cap, only the brown locks at the back and a little at the sides could be seen.

"Hmm… Maybe I do, maybe I don't and *maybe* I'm a nice stranger," he replied, smiling a little.

"Nice try. Didn't your parents tell you not to talk to strangers?"

"They probably did but I usually tuned out so I may have missed that part, if I'm being completely honest." She chuckled in response before rolling her eyes and adjusting her glasses. "OK, I'll let you read in peace. Nice talking to you, new girl," he finished and left her to it.

About half an hour later, she began to pack up her stuff after her eyes had become tired with all of the reading she had done. The cafe was quiet with only a handful of people left which was a change from the usual madness. She felt weird, like she was being watched. She slowly lifted her head and scanned the room; no one was looking at her apart from one person. She got butterflies in her stomach just by looking at him. That wasn't good, considering she was married.

"Are you done?" she shouted over to Tyler who was standing in his usual spot behind the cash register.

"Done with?" he questioned, raising his eyebrows.

"Staring me out, jeez," she replied, before drinking the last of her drink which was cold as she had forgotten about it.

He laughed. "I only just looked up; I have no clue what you're talking about," he said, shrugging his shoulders and smirking a little.

The corners of her mouth curled into a smile as she rolled her eyes once again. He made her smile, that was for sure. He walked over to where she was packing up and started to pick up her mug and clean the mess she had made when she spilled a couple of drops of her drink.

"Wow, at least I got a smile out of you," he continued, laughing lightly.

"I actually always smile, so shut up," she scowled and continued doing what she was doing.

"Hm, OK but you are hard to talk to."

"I'm talking now, aren't I?"

"Yeah but I want you to really talk to me."

"Yeahhhhh, that's not gonna happen. Sorry buddy."

"You know you want to though. I mean, how can you not want to talk to this face?" He gave her his best puppy dog eyes to which she laughed and shook her head.

"Wow, cocky. OK. I think that's my cue to leave. Bye stranger," she said.

She flung her bag over her shoulder and swivelled her heels, ready to leave. Just as she did, he called after her.

"Wait, so uh, see you tomorrow?" he asked, wishing more than anything that she would say yes.

"Maybe you will, maybe you won't," she replied as she opened the cafe door.

"What did you say your name was?" he asked, he needed that at least.

"I didn't," she said and with that she was gone.

Chapter Nine

The room was full of rich lawyers and their plus ones. They chatted, they laughed and they sipped champagne as they socialised. They were all dressed to perfection, full of elegance and class. She didn't fit in there at all but Brad did and he was the reason that she was there as it was his work night out. She thought that it would have been a dinner or something but the full on party that they were at, was far from it. She did not want to be there at all but she just had to get over it, put on a smile and make it through the night. She and Brad got themselves a drink and headed over to where a smart looking Joe stood.

"Hey guys!" Joe greeted them as they joined him. Joe was one of Brad's good friends and also worked with him. He was actually a really nice guy and liked to share the odd joke every now and again.

"Hey Joe. How are you?" Holly replied and flashed a smile.

"Very well, thank you. I was just talking about you, Brad."

"Oh, you were?" Brad asked, his eyebrows raised slightly as he took a sip of his drink.

"Yeah, buddy, me and the guys were just talking about how you're such a handful at times," Joe joked, grinning at Brad. Joe knew how much high maintenance Brad could be at times.

"Me, a handful? Never!" Brad said as he shook his head lightly.

"Honestly, Holly, I don't know how you put up with him," Joe continued.

"Me neither, Joe. You think he's bad at work, you should see him at home! A NIGHTMARE!" Holly spoke, chuckling a little with Joe.

Joe probably thought she was joking but she really wasn't. He was a nightmare. Her marriage was a nightmare. Although he forced a laugh, she could feel Brad's eyes fixed on her as if to say, "Why did you say that?" and she didn't dare turn to look at him as she was afraid he would be full of rage. It was getting to the point where she was getting tired of holding her tongue and he was getting angry so easily. All they ever did was fight. She couldn't even remember the last time he genuinely made her smile or laugh or just made her feel good. She just wished he would get sick of her, sign the papers and let her be free.

For the rest of the night, they continued to mingle and it seemed like Brad had forgotten about her earlier comment as he never said anything about it to her. Instead, he was talking to her briefly about other things. He continued to flash smiles and make conversation with all of his friends and associates, having the time of his life. She felt so relieved because if he was in a good mood then it meant that she was safe.

***

When they arrived home that night, they were both sat on the sofa, unwinding after their long evening out. Brad was engrossed in the T.V. and Holly was just flicking through her phone, in her own little world. She was so glad to be home, away from everyone. She was getting so bored of making small talk at the party with people who hardly made an effort back, except from a few people. The more uncomfortable she was getting at the party, the more comfortable he was getting and she practically had to drag him out when she just couldn't bear it any more.

"Holly," Brad spoke, finally interested in something other than the T.V.

"Yeah?" Holly replied as she put her phone down and looked directly at him.

"You know, you acted like a brat today," he scolded her, the tone of his voice stern.

"I did?" she asked, she knew exactly what he was referring to but she technically didn't say anything wrong.

"You called me a nightmare, in front of Joe."

"You are. Don't worry, he thought I was joking. Didn't you hear him laughing?"

"I am actually getting quite sick of your childish behaviour. You're such a disgrace. I give you everything. I bought you this massive house. I let you quit your job so you could have it easy. Honestly, other people would be so happy but here you are full of attitude. Not to mention, you are actually being rude."

"Well if you're getting sick of me then JUST GIVE ME THAT DIVORCE I ASKED FOR!" she yelled, getting up and beginning to walk away. Her hands were shaking slightly because that was the first time she had ever dared to yell at him like that.

"EXCUSE ME?" Brad called after her, irritated with her yelling.

She ignored him and continued to walk away. He followed her quickly, not making a sound and grabbed her hair when he was near enough. She let out a scream and began squirming, trying to free herself from him. He was strong and his grip was so tight that her efforts were, of course, unsuccessful. He pulled her hair as hard as he could; it was her punishment for acting so silly.

"What do you say?" he questioned her, still pulling at her hair. She kept quiet, not wanting to give in to his foolishness. A few tears rolled down her cheeks after she closed her eyes firmly, desperate for him to just leave her alone and let go. Refusing to give up, he yanked her head back and forth by her hair until she caved.

"OK, I'm sorry. Please will you let me go?" she begged, the pain was becoming so unbearable so she had to say what he wanted her to.

He let go of her hair once she apologised and threw a few strands of her hair that had come out, on the floor.

"Was that really so hard? Just remember, all of this could have been avoided if you just acted like a normal human being instead of being so bitter and moody all the time," he finished. He rolled his eyes and made a swift exit out of the hallway, leaving her alone to cry silently.

Chapter Ten

She opened the doors to the cafe and the smell of freshly baked cake hit her at once. She inhaled the smell, savouring it because she knew she wasn't going to have any. She looked around the place as she walked over to the counter. It was a busy afternoon in the cafe, some people deep in conversation while others had their heads buried in books or magazines. Despite the cafe being so busy, her usual seat was surprisingly empty like it had been saved just for her. She smiled slightly, the place made her happy. It had a certain warmth and homely feel to it which she loved and it just had so many positives vibes. It was quickly becoming her favourite place to go. A place that lifted her spirits, with the help of the friendly staff, a certain guy in particular. A place where she felt safe. A place where she could forget about all of her troubles, even if was just for a while.

"Fancy seeing you here again!" Tyler chirped and gave her a wink as she got to the front of the queue.

She rolled her eyes at him but couldn't help a smile from forming on her face. "Hey Tyler!" she greeted him, placing her bag on the counter.

"Hey, how are you?"

"I'm OK, how are you?"

"I'm great now," he smirked before chuckling a little.

"Oh god, you just don't give up do you?" They both laughed. "So, tell me, do you flirt with every girl that comes in here?" she continued and folded her arms as she waited for a response.

"*Well*... No, I'm kidding! Only a certain pretty brunette that caught my eye the first time she came in here," he smiled.

"Oh, is that right?" she asked, now it was her who was smirking a little.

"Mmhmm."

"You're crazy."

"You love it," he teased before fixing the collar of his navy-blue polo shirt.

"*Well*..." she mimicked before laughing.

"You want your usual?" he asked, holding up a mug.

"Yeah, please," she said. She pulled out her purse, gave him the money and turned to go to her seat.

"If you need company, just call me over," he called behind her and she laughed.

"I'll keep that in mind," she replied when she faced him after taking her seat.

She spent the next half an hour sipping away at her coffee and reading her book which was very addictive. She had been in her own world, not really noticing what anyone else was doing. She peered over her book and took a look to see what was going on around her. There was a family of four sitting near her and it was the first time she had noticed them. They looked like the perfect family. The mother and father were both dressed very nicely as were their children. The father wore a khaki coloured sweater with black jeans and the mother had a black fitted dress on which she teamed with black heels and a white Céline bag. Her thick, brown hair sat perfectly in loose curls as she attended to her children. The couple had two children, a girl and a boy, both extremely cute. They both had glasses but were the complete opposite in other ways, from what she could see. The little girl, who had her hair in neat French plaits, was telling her parents a story. Her hands were moving as she told it, various expressions appearing on her face. The curly haired little boy sat quietly at the table drawing on a piece of paper, not interested in the girl's story.

Holly had always hoped that Brad would change his mind about having kids and that they would have a whole bunch of them but judging by the way things were going, that was very unlikely. Her smile faded when she started to think about her life and she decided to turn her attention elsewhere. Tyler came into her view and instantly put a smile back on her face. He was busy joking around with an elderly woman who was laughing at whatever he was saying. He looked up from the woman and realised that Holly was watching him. She turned a light shade of pink and quickly looked back at her book, trying to hide her embarrassment.

About ten minutes later, Tyler was walking around the cafe. He was attending to a few things and was chatting to the occasional customer. She saw him from the corner of her eye and thought she would use the opportunity to ask him about the wi-fi.

"Tyler," she called as she turned around in her chair.

"Give me two seconds," he replied, finishing what he was doing.

A few moments later, he appeared at her table, full of smiles. "You OK?" he asked.

"Yeah, I'm fine thanks. I just wanted to ask if you have wi-fi in here."

"Yeah, we do. I'll put it in for you," he suggested, holding out his hand. She handed her phone to him and let him put the password in.

"Thank you," she said as she took her phone back and gave him a soft smile.

"You owe me," he joked, a small grin on his face.

"What can I do to repay you, Tyler?"

"Nothing, I was just kidding. *Actually*, there is something," he laughed and sat on the arm rest of her chair.

"What?" she questioned, looking up at him.

"OK, so you didn't tell me your story which was fair enough, we'll get there one day. So, how about your name?"

"Hmm…" Holly pondered; surely it wouldn't be that bad if she gave just her name. It wasn't like he would be able find out her deepest and darkest secrets with it.

"Oh, come on," he begged.

"Holly," she finally said.

He gazed at her as though he was trying to register the name with her face. "Holly," he repeated. "No surname?"

"Just Holly."

"OK, 'just Holly'. We're getting somewhere." He lifted up his hand and gave her a high five before continuing, "I have another thing that you can do actually."

"Go on."

"A date."

"With me?" She guffawed and shook her head.

"No, sorry I'm just talking to that lady over there," he said, the sarcasm clear in his voice. He nodded to the woman who was sitting behind her and they both shared a giggle. "Of course I'm talking about you!" he confirmed and looked directly at her as he eagerly awaited a response.

This was horrible for Holly. She wanted more than anything to say yes and agree to his offer because she did actually enjoy his company but the situation with Brad was lingering over her. It was like a dull cloud hanging over her, making her miserable. She was scared that he would find out somehow but then again, she could just be careful. She hesitated for a while, the thoughts circling around in her head.

"So, this date... What does it entail exactly?" she quizzed him.

"How about; me and you, a burger and fries *and* a nice drive? I'm a low-key kinda guy," he proposed and nervously shook his leg.

She gave it a thought. Maybe it wouldn't be so bad, it was only a drive after all and they could go somewhere away from her home.

"Well, you're lucky I'm a low-key kinda girl then aren't you?" she said and put her hand on his leg to stop him from shaking it.

"See, I knew you couldn't resist the charm," he joked and a faint smirk appeared on his face. "Tomorrow then? The usual time you come in?"

"You're on." She flashed him a smile and gave him another high five.

Chapter Eleven

She collapsed onto her bed, so many clothes spread out beside her. She had given up. She couldn't find anything to wear for the date and it was beginning to give her anxiety. She was even thinking about calling him and just cancelling, that's how done she was but she remembered that she didn't have his number so that wasn't an option. She just couldn't find the right top to wear and by the looks of it, she was going to be late if she didn't hurry up. She mustered up the courage and stood up; ready to look again otherwise she really would be late. After fifteen minutes of searching, she finally went with a black turtleneck, black jeans and a pair of black boots. All black but she was past caring. She tied up her hair into a tight ponytail, the waves still intact and put on a pair of silver hooped earrings. Her make-up was already done so she was all ready to go. She threw her bag on her forearm and ran out of the house, hoping to not be late.

He sat at the cafe twiddling his thumbs, unsure of whether she was going to show or not. It wouldn't surprise him if she didn't show and had changed her mind; she was way out of his league. He really hoped that she would show though because he was keen to spend time with her and get to know her. She was a sweet girl but she was very guarded and there was something about that, that he was attracted to. There was so much more of her he still had to figure out but he was ready for it. He was about to pull out his phone and call her when he realised her didn't have her number.

"Hey Bob," he called to the chef, leaning against the doorframe of the kitchen.

"What's up kid?" Bob replied, a dish towel over his shoulder.

Bob had been the chef at the cafe since the place opened and he and Tyler had quickly become good friends. Bob was like a father figure to him which he needed as his own father had abandoned him and his elder sister when they were just kids. Bob was the one he went to when he needed advice or anything and Bob treated him as if he was his own son. He was such a friendly guy with such a big heart and Tyler was always thankful for him.

"Do you think she will show?" Tyler quizzed him.

"One hundred percent" Bob confirmed as he cracked a few eggs into a bowl.

"You think so?" An intrigued look appeared on Tyler's face.

"I know so, Ty," Bob reassured, nodding towards the door of the cafe with a grin on his face.

Tyler spun around and now he had a grin on his face. She had arrived. She actually showed up and she looked so beautiful. She always did.

***

They sat in his matte, gunmetal, grey Mercedes, both eating their burgers. He was probably enjoying his more than she was considering the fact that the only thing that was on her mind was that she wanted to be sick after eating. She just had to eat, get through the date and let it out later. She glanced over at Tyler after she ate a couple of fries and he just looked so adorable with the napkin spread across his legs to make sure he didn't ruin his jeans.

"You liking it?" he asked once he finished the food in his mouth.

"So good. I'm just so full though," she lied. She couldn't bring herself to eat any more and not be sick so she stopped after her last bite. "You look like you're enjoying yours!" she continued, laughing while gesturing towards the empty box on his laps.

"There's something you should know about me. I love my food," he confessed, holding up his hands.

"Fatty," she teased, smiling softly.

They both chuckled. "So, Holly, tell me something – Why here?" he questioned and turned in his seat to look at her properly.

"Huh?" she said, unaware of what he was talking about.

"Why did you pick here to move to? I mean it's not exactly the greatest of places."

"I actually love this place, you know. But yeah, it wasn't my first choice. I just needed somewhere to start afresh and someone suggested this place."

"Ah, OK. What was your first choice?"

"New York City. Well that's more of a dream really. I would love to move there one day and live in a cosy apartment that overlooks Central Park."

"What's stopping you?"

"Uh... Timing."

He noticed the dull look on her face and instantly felt bad for asking but decided to continue anyway. "What's the apartment like?"

"It's up high. Just two bedrooms but there's an extra small room that I can use to do my writing. The room has a desk and a swivel chair and there is a bookshelf against the wall for all of my books. The room is black and white. The bedroom is grey and white with a few pillows on the bed and a soft grey carpet," she told him, her face lighting up as she spoke about her dream apartment.

"Wow, you have it all figured out, huh?" he said with an impressed look on his face.

"Yeah. One day."

"One day," he repeated before stopping for a minute. "Wait, you write?"

"I do," she beamed.

"That's awesome. What kind of stuff do you write?"

"Mostly short stories. It's so therapeutic for me."

"Have you published any?"

She shook her head vigorously. "Oh no. They aren't that good!"

"Don't be silly, you should give it a go. You never know," he said before putting his seatbelt on and getting ready to drive again.

For the rest of the date, they conversed and they laughed. There was no awkwardness or struggling to make conversation and honestly it was like they had known each other for ages. She just didn't want it to end and she didn't want to go back home where everything was miserable. She wanted to press pause and enjoy the day forever. She was really enjoying his company and was beginning to find herself becoming more and more attracted to him compared to when she first met him. His cockiness made her weary when she first met him but she was starting to realise that there was so much more to him than that and that she had him all figured out wrong. The car came to a halt as he parked up across from the cafe.

"Have you had a good time?" he asked her as he opened a bar of chocolate. "Honestly?"

"You know what, this was such a simple date but I loved it," she gushed. He had a smug look on his face after he heard what she said. "The company could have been better though," she joked and he gave her a look before laughing. "I feel like all we've done is talk about me though. Tell me about yourself," she continued.

"What do you wanna know?" he asked before drinking his juice.

"Anything." She spoke softly, gazing at him.

"My name's Tyler and I'm twenty-six years old," he laughed. She rolled her eyes at his comment and let out a laugh. "OK, seriously?" he said, being serious.

"Seriously," she nodded her head and he continued.

"OK, well you've probably figured out that I own that place, hence my name on the sign." He pointed to the cafe. "I've had it for about four years now and I love it. I don't actually need to work there because I have staff obviously but I choose to because I like being there and watching the place grow."

"You're cute."

"Thank you." He blushed. "You want the rest?" he asked her, holding up the chocolate bar and she shook her head in response. "What else? Erm... I went to USC and studied mechanical engineering. Oh, one of my biggest passions in life is cars. I love to drive them, I love to fix them and I love to work with them. Just anything to do with cars, I love," he finished with a smile on his face.

"Ah, I love that. Never had you down for that though."

"That's the thing, 'just Holly'. There's more to me than what meets the eye. Stick around for a while and you'll find out yourself."

"And I thought that I was the mysterious one! Well, I'm not going anywhere anytime soon so I look forward to figuring you out."

"Likewise, Holly. Likewise."

She looked at him and let a smile form on her face as she noticed that he had some chocolate on the corner of his mouth. Without any hesitation, she moved closer to him and reached over to wipe it away with her thumb. She met his eyes a moment after that, her hand still on his face and let herself get lost in them. They both let themselves get lost in the moment. Neither of them spoke until Holly cleared her throat and dropped her hand, her heart beating fast. She returned to her normal position and Tyler lowered his gaze at once.

"Uh, we should go. I need to get back home," she blurted, breaking the silence between them before glancing at her watch.

"Yeah, w — we should," he stuttered, his nerves taking over.

Before she climbed out of the car, she looked around outside to see if anyone was around and squeezed his arm gently. "Thank you for today. I had a really nice time," she said.

"Anytime. Will I see you tomorrow?" he asked.

"Yeah, see you then." She flashed him a smile which he returned and got out of the car.

***

Back at home that evening, Holly put chicken into a pan and began to make Brad's dinner. She was so glad that she had made it home before he did otherwise he would have started asking questions and the last thing that she needed was him becoming suspicious. The whole time she had been home, the only thing she could think about was Tyler and how much fun she had. It was the first time in a while that she had laughed and smiled so much and it was so exhilarating. She loved how he actually paid attention to her and was interested in her interests. He listened to everything that she had to say which was a lot different than what Brad would ever do. After a while of them being together, Brad started to brush her interests aside and somehow make it all about him. She knew deep down that her friendship with Tyler could never progress to anything more because, of course, she was married. However, she just wanted to enjoy being in his company for the time being. She truly felt like a schoolgirl when she was around him, that's how much she was starting to like him.

Brad walked into the kitchen and noticed the smile on his wife's face as she cooked away. He wondered why she was so happy.

"Why are you so happy today?" he asked as he washed his hands.

"What?" she asked, her smile fading at once.

"You seemed very happy there. I was just wondering what the reason was."

"Oh, no reason," she lied.

"Oh. Well less smiling and more cooking. I'm hungry," he demanded and left her to it, walking back out of the kitchen.

"Of course," she said quietly.

Chapter Twelve

Months passed since her date with Tyler and she found herself falling in love with him. The more time that they spent together, the more intense her feelings for him became and the more she continued to lose interest in Brad. At this point, he was just someone who she shared a house with. She had been seeing Tyler almost every afternoon and it was great. They were growing closer and closer as time went on. She still hadn't told him about Brad but she knew that she would have to sooner or later.

She sat at the cafe, thinking about how different her life would have been if she wasn't married. She would have been able to do so much more with Tyler, like day trips that he had suggested before but she had to shoot him down. If only the timing was different and the situation was different.

"Hey, Hol." Tyler interrupted her daydream, tilting his head to try and get her attention.

"Sorry. I was just thinking about stuff," she replied, turning her attention to the blue-eyed boy who was sitting next to her on the sofa.

"It's OK. You look cute daydreaming," he said, tucking a strand of her hair behind her ear. She blushed a little in response to his statement and rested her head on his shoulder. He put his arm around her and moved closer to her.

"Can I tell you something?" she asked, looking up at him.

"Of course," he replied.

"I have loved every minute I have spent with you," she confessed and gave him a half smile.

He smiled softly and kissed the top of her head. "That's cute."

She lifted up her head and looked out of the window that was on her right and she froze for a moment. She sat up abruptly and moved Tyler's arm away from her. She was so sure that she had seen Brad walking on the sidewalk and she was freaking out, her heart beating at what felt like 100mph. After a few minutes of looking outside intensely, she realised that it wasn't actually him but she was still so terrified.

"What's wrong with you?" Tyler questioned, moving forward so he was aligned with her.

"Nothing," she lied. She gulped, she was freaked out. Maybe that was a sign that she had to stop messing about. She got her bag and stood up. "I need to go now. I'm sorry," she said.

"Wait, Hol, what happened?" he called after her, a confused look on his face but he got no response as she made a swift exit from the cafe.

Chapter Thirteen

After a very sleepless night, she was awake. When she checked the time, she could have cried. It was only nine a.m. and after tossing and turning the whole night and hardly sleeping, it wasn't ideal. Her mind had been so occupied with so many thoughts; thoughts about Tyler and how risky it was for her to be hanging out with him. She had to tell him as soon as she could, she knew she had to. She had been rehearsing how to tell him and the more she thought about it all, the more sick she was starting to feel. She wished more than anything that she didn't have to tell him but she just had to put her feelings aside and do it. Today was the day that she was going to tell him but she couldn't get away with going early afternoon while Brad was working because Tyler wasn't at the cafe till late afternoon. She wanted to talk to him properly so she knew that it was going to take time and by that time Brad would be home so she had told Brad that she was going to the gym in the evening so that she would still be able to get out. He was OK with her going to the gym because he wanted her to go and lose weight. In his eyes, she was too fat even though she was actually a normal size.

For the rest of the morning and early afternoon, she kept herself busy doing chores around the house.

She had hoped that it would keep her mind off the situation with Tyler but it didn't work. The thoughts were lingering and they were breaking her heart. When she had finished her chores, she glanced at the clock in the living room and a look of relief flickered over her face as she realised it was four-thirty p.m. and she could finally go and get it over with. The relief only lasted a second and sadness took over when she remembered that it would be the last time she would ever see Tyler.

She sat in a small room at the back of the cafe, anxiously biting her nails. Tyler was running late so Bob had suggested that she could wait in there if she wanted to when he realised that her and Tyler's conversation was going to be a serious one. The look on her face had given it away. She began pacing back and forth around the room and the sick feeling in the pit of her stomach had returned, more prominent than ever. She scanned the room, taking in her surroundings and noticed a few bookshelves in the corner filled with many books. She decided to wander over in the hope that maybe a book would occupy her mind for the time being. Tyler entered the room a few minutes later and spotted her, with her back to the door, flicking through a book from his collection. It seemed that she was that engrossed in it or in her thoughts that she hadn't even realised he had come in. He walked over behind her and lightly squeezed her shoulders, before wrapping his arms around her and resting his chin on her head.

"Hey babe," he spoke softly as she turned her head to see him.

"Hey," she said and placed the book back on the shelf. She placed her hand on his arm that was still wrapped around her and caressed it with her thumb. She leaned into him for a few moments, enjoying his embrace before she broke it and turned around to face him.

"You look cute," she continued, giving him a warm smile which he returned. "You OK?"

"I'm so sleepy. Other than that, I'm good. What about you?" he asked and took a seat on the armrest of the sofa that was behind him.

She gulped and a lump began to form in her throat as she looked at his tired but sweet face. Her eyes started to well-up at once and she quickly swivelled around so that she was facing the bookshelf again and buried her head in her hands, sobbing quietly.

"Hey, hey, hey," he consoled and wrapped her in a tight hug. "What's up?"

Unable to speak, she sank into him and allowed her head to fall slightly onto his chest. She continued to sob, his t-shirt beginning to become a little wet from all of the tears.

"Is this to do with what happened the other day? Your sudden exit?" he continued, pulling her away from him so he could see her face. She nodded, wiped her tears, took a deep breath and managed to stop crying.

"Yeah, it's about that. I need to speak to you," she mumbled.

"What happened?"

"This thing that we have got going on. I can't do it any more, I'm sorry."

"Wait, what?" he asked, clearly confused about her random outburst when things were going so well between them.

"I thought we were having fun and enjoying hanging out?"

"I was. It's just complicated and I can't get into it but I just think it's best we don't see each other anymore." She replied, her heart breaking at the sight of the sad look on his face.

"Uh, babe, where is this coming from?" he enquired with his eyebrows furrowed.

"I'm sorry. I need to go," she blurted nervously.

"OK, you can go but first tell me why you're so scared," he insisted. He was concerned about her state.

"Scared? I never said I was scared."

"You didn't have to, Hol. Your face says it all. What is it that's so bad that it's making you feel like this, huh?"

"It's complicated."

"Oh. You wanna shut me out, fine. Just know that I care about you, a lot, and I'm worried about you. Are you OK? Like honestly? You're not in any kind of trouble, are you?" he questioned, his voice filled with concern.

He cared so much about her and it was the sweetest thing ever. She hesitated before responding to him. She wanted more than anything to tell him and began pacing again. He was such a good guy and he deserved to know the truth but she was still contemplating. Just knowing that he had her best interests at heart made her heart sink a little.

"Hol?" he said and put his hand on her arm to stop her pacing.

"Sorry. What were you saying?" she muttered.

"You in trouble?"

"No, no. No trouble."

"You promise?"

She found herself hesitating again. She didn't want to keep lying through her teeth. *"Would it be the worst thing in the world if I just told him?"* she thought to herself as she looked at Tyler, who was desperately waiting for an answer.

"Look, there's got to be a reason why you keep hesitating. What is it?" he continued.

"I just can't do this anymore."

"But why? We are just two single people enjoying each other's company. Did I do something wrong?"

She shook her head. "That's the thing. I might be enjoying your company a little too much. The more time I spend with you, the more I fall in love with you and it's breaking my heart," she sobbed, wiping away her tears as they escaped her eyes.

"You're in love with me?" he said softly, his eyes widening.

"I'm sorry, this was a bad idea. Forget I said anything." She turned to walk out of the door but stopped when he stood up and grasped her wrist gently.

"Hey, wait. What's so wrong with that? I love you too, you know that," he confirmed and wiped away the last of her tears.

"It just can't work, OK?"

"Look, I don't know what's going on with you right now but I want nothing more than to give this a go. Give me one good reason why this won't wor —"

"I'm married," she blurted, cutting him off.

His face dropped and he looked even more confused than he did before. "You're what?" he questioned. He jumped out of his seat and looked at her intensely.

"Married."

"Nah, you've got to be joking. There's no way you're married. Good one though," he chuckled and sat back down.

"I'm serious, Tyler. His name's Brad, he's a lawyer," she said.

"Well, where's the ring?"

"I take it off when I'm out." She rummaged through her bag and held up the ring that sparkled as the sunlight hit it.

"Wow." He rubbed his eyes and tried to digest that she wasn't joking.

"I'm so sorry. I should have told you sooner."

"Why didn't you tell me? Why have you been hanging out with me and getting close to me when you're married?"

"Because it's not like that with him. I'm just married to him. That's it. There's no feelings there, not anymore."

"OK, so leave him if you don't love him."

"I can't."

"What do you mean, you can't? File for divorce."

"He's abusive, Ty. He won't let me leave," she cried.

"He hurt you?" he said, his voice raising and the anger building up inside of him at the thought of some guy hurting someone who was so precious to him.

The sight of her standing there with tears streaming down her face made it so much harder for him to not be angry. He took a few minutes to get himself together. The last thing she needed was him acting like an idiot so he had to calm down. He walked over to her and wrapped her in a tight hug. He dropped one hand and rubbed her back, trying to console her.

"I'm so sorry," she sobbed, clinging to him.

"Hey," he comforted her. "You have nothing to apologise for. It's him that's going to be sorry. I'm going to call the police." He reached into his pocket for his cell phone before she stopped him.

"You can't. That will make things worse. Please don't do anything," she pleaded and held down his arm so he couldn't get to his phone.

"Are you serious? I can't just not do anything. He needs to pay for what he's doing to you."

"Babe. Please. We don't have any proof anyway. I've thought about it before, trust me."

"I'm not gonna let him hurt you and get away with it."

"You have to. If he finds out that I've been sneaking around, he will be mad. He's horrible when he's mad. So, so horrible."

"So, you just expect me to let you go back there and suffer? You want me to let you just walk away?" he asked, his face glum.

"Yeah," she said quietly. She looked up at him and cupped his cheek with her hand. "Thank you for reminding me what love felt like. You will always have such a special place in my heart and I will always, always love you. You know that, right?" she continued, blinking back her tears.

It was one of the hardest things she had ever had to do. He nodded and placed his hand over hers that was still placed on his cheek.

"I'm sorry but I can't just pretend that I don't know anything. There's gotta be another way," he insisted.

"There's not. I can't see you again. It's too risky and it's not fair on you either. You deserve someone much better who will give you all of her attention and love you in ways I'm not able to," she said. Her heart was hurting so bad.

"Look." He paused and rummaged around in the drawer of the desk. "Here's a spare phone. My number is in there, use it to call me and check in when you can. Just five minutes, I just need to know you're OK."

"He's going to find this," she spoke, holding up the phone.

"He won't. Just be careful and it'll be fine," he reassured.

"Thank you," she said, giving him one last hug before she had to leave. "Ty?"

He looked at her and nodded for her to continue. "If you don't hear from me for a while then it probably means that he found out, so if it comes to that then please, please, please don't wait for me," she begged as she brushed away the tear that fell from her eye.

"You're mad. I'm going to wait for you, no matter how long it takes," he confessed, giving her arm a gentle squeeze.

Chapter Fourteen

She got home later that evening and she was still a mess. She didn't want to be home at all. All she wanted was to go back to him; her happy place. She popped her head round the living room door and saw Brad sitting with his back to her, busy taking a phone call. She decided to use the opportunity to go and freshen up before he started asking questions. Before she started with all of that, she remembered that she still had Tyler's phone in her pocket. She quickly took it and buried it at the bottom of her handbag. Brad would never check there as he never went through or touched her bags.

Downstairs, Brad sat deep in thought. The more he thought about a certain situation, the angrier he was getting. Earlier, when he had finished work, he decided to swing by the gym that Holly had said that she was going to as he liked to keep tabs on her. However, there was no sign of her there which was weird because he was there at the time she had given him so she should have been there. He had got back into his car and was ready to go home but then curiosity got the better of him. He decided to go back into the gym to ask if she had been in at all as she could have gone earlier. To his disappointment, the receptionist had said that she hadn't been there at any point during the day. That meant only one thing, Holly had lied to him and it enraged him. *"Who does she think is and, more importantly, where had she really been?"* he thought to himself. He jumped up off of the sofa and went to confront her about the whole situation.

He entered his bedroom to find it empty which puzzled him until he realised that the bathroom light was on. He took a seat at the edge of the bed and loosened his tie. He moved his foot slightly and accidently knocked over her bag that was lying on the floor. He bent down and began picking up the stuff that had fallen out and putting it back in when he noticed something strange. There was an old phone that lay on the floor. He knew at once that it wasn't Holly's as she had a newer phone. A look of confusion flickered over his face before he confirmed to himself that something was definitely going on. He picked up the phone and pressed the home button.

"Hol. Are you OK?" The message read from someone called Tyler.

Finally, it all made sense. The lies, the distance she had been keeping from him, the extra phone. It all added up now; she was having an affair. His blood was boiling as he realised what was going on right under his nose. He was about to show her that she had made a mistake messing with him. A big mistake.

A few minutes later, she emerged from the bathroom and noticed that Brad had come upstairs. What she didn't notice though, was that he knew everything because he had placed the phone into his pocket and was acting normal.

"Hi Holly," Brad said as he took off his watch and placed it on the bedside cabinet.

"Hi," she responded dryly, taking a seat at her dressing table.

"How's your day been? How was the gym?" he asked.

She gulped. "Yeah, it was good," she lied as she picked up the moisturiser that was lying on the dressing table in front of her.

"YOU LIAR!" he yelled and threw Tyler's phone with such force that it smashed the mirror she was sitting in front of, pieces of glass falling everywhere.

She gasped and dropped what she was holding. "No, no, no, no," she cried as he stormed over to her, full of rage.

A look of fear was plastered on her face as she watched him. "I gave you a chance to come clean. You stupid, stupid girl. This is all happening because of you. Look how angry you have made me!" he hissed and slapped her face hard.

Unable to say anything, she touched her cheek where it hurt and cried. Her breathing quickened and she began trembling with fear.

"Oh, Tyler messaged. He wants to know if you're OK," he laughed.

"I — I can explain," she mumbled.

"No need. From now on, you will do exactly as I say and you will not be going out any more. Got it?" he demanded, glaring down at her. "Oh and you're a pathetic wife. You'll need to work on that," he finished, left the room and stormed down the stairs.

She froze. She just lay there, unable to move or speak. She wished more than anything that this nightmare would stop already. Her breathing began to slow down and the tears stopped but she was still stuck in shock. She was traumatised as she lay there curled up into a ball, silently praying for a way out.

Chapter Fifteen

Two years later.

Two years later and she was still dealing with the same crap. She was married to a monster but someone else had her heart. Her marriage was a mess. Brad still wasn't willing to get a divorce and her life was as miserable as it could get. He loved the fact that she was so terrified of him. They barely even acknowledged each other anymore. If Brad did speak to her, it was always some sort of horrible comment because he had nothing nice to say to her. She took it; she took everything because she had no other choice. That was until today. She had made a plan, she wasn't sure if it would work or not but it was worth a shot. Her plan consisted of setting up a camera somewhere and catching him beating her, without him knowing, of course, and then she would have evidence that she could take to the police. If it worked, she could finally have her life back and be free from the horrible nightmare that she was trapped in.

Brad tucked into his dinner, not saying a word to her. She played around with her food, not in the mood to eat anything. She was feeling very anxious about her plan and if it would work or not but she had to stay optimistic and hold onto the smallest glimmer of hope that she did have. She had hidden the camera in one of the shelves in the kitchen earlier in the day. She was sure something would happen for him to snap because these days it was so easy to trigger his violence. He noticed how she was just playing with her food and not eating anything. She got up from the table and emptied her plate into the trash can.

"That's good," he said as he watched her.

"What?" she said quietly, putting her dishes in the sink.

"Not eating the lasagne. You could do with something healthier." He sniggered and patted his stomach.

"You know what, I am so sick of your stupid comments. It wouldn't hurt to say something nice for once. All you do is treat me like crap," she snapped, slamming her glass on the counter.

"I treat you like crap? OK. What about the car I got you, the shoes, and the bags? Look at all the things I provide for you and I treat you like crap? OK," he snapped, putting down his fork and scraping back his chair.

"That's the thing, Brad. I never wanted any of that. All I ever wanted was your love and your time. These past few years, you haven't been able to give me either of those things."

"I come home to you every night, don't I? Is that not enough? I could easily stay out and not bother coming back to you. I could cheat on you if I wanted to, but have I? No."

"You might as well have," she spat and turned around to continue with what she was doing.

"You better watch your tone, lady," he hissed.

"Or what?" she retorted. She knew exactly what was coming but for once, she needed it to happen.

"THIS IS WHAT," he yelled, dragging her through the kitchen by the hair.

He continued to abuse her and hit her multiple times. She took it and suffered in silence but it was OK because she knew that was it. The end was near. Once he was finished with her, for the first ever time ever, she lay there and smiled through the pain.

***

The next morning, she woke up feeling happy for once. Her plan the night before had worked and she couldn't believe it. This was her last morning in the house because she didn't want to waste any time. She got out of bed, freshened up and began packing all of her stuff. She was only taking the stuff that she bought herself as she didn't want anything that was from him. She didn't want any reminder of him whatsoever. She took off her wedding ring and placed it on Brad's bedside table and it felt so good. Once she had finished packing all of her stuff, she picked up the camera and off she went.

Elsewhere, Tyler flicked through the papers one last time before handing them to Bob. He still couldn't believe the fact that he was selling the cafe but he knew that it was what he had to do for his future. He wasn't going to be in Morro Bay much, especially if Holly came back to him. He had it all planned out. He grabbed his car keys and just as he was about to leave, the cafe door swung open and he couldn't believe his eyes. She stood there looking so broken, still beautiful, but broken and he hated him for it. She stood still and took in the sight of him standing there in front of the counter, the same place she saw him for the first time. All it took was one look at him and all the feelings came flooding back. Her stomach filled with butterflies and her heart skipped a beat. Two years later and she was still so in love with him. She dropped her bag and she ran to him. He scooped her up and gave her one of the biggest hugs ever. Neither of them spoke, instead they just enjoyed each other's embrace and enjoyed the moment that they had both been longing for. She shuddered at first because she was a little sore from the night before but he then loosened his grip. She felt so safe in his arms and it was everything that she had been wishing for.

"Hi!" she blurted, pulling away to look at him.

"Uh, hi!" he replied. He was still getting over the fact that she was actually there and that he wasn't dreaming. "You're back!" he exclaimed with a big smile on his face.

She nodded and she too, had a big smile on her face. "How?" he asked.

"I got out, Ty. I finally got out," she replied. She beamed with pride as she realised that she actually did it and she became filled with relief.

"Won't he come looking for you? Is it safe for you to be here?"

"The police are dealing with it so it will be fine," she reassured him.

A look of relief flickered over his face. He put his hand on her cheek and smiled softly at her. He was so proud of her and how she had managed to stay strong and get herself out.

"You don't know how happy I am right now, Hol. I have been dreaming of this moment for the past two years."

"Me too, babe. Me too."

They sat on the sofa in the empty cafe and it was the first time Holly had seen it so quiet. There was not a single person in sight, apart from the two of them.

"Hey, what's happened to this place? Why is it so quiet?" she asked, filled with curiosity.

"Oh, we are closed today. I just came in to sign the papers. I'm selling," he clarified, taking a look around the place.

"What? Why? You love this place," she said.

"I have plans, you'll see. You'll see." He looked at her lovingly, so happy that he finally had her back.

She met his gaze and blushed slightly. "So, uh… you seeing anyone?" she questioned, desperately hoping that his answer would be what she wanted to hear.

"Well, there's this girl that I'm mad about and I think we're just going to take it slow and see where it goes," he babbled with a hint of a smile on his face.

Her face dropped at once. "Oh. Are you happy?"

"Yeah, I am," he laughed, putting his feet up on the table.

"Why are you laughing?"

"The girl I'm talking about is you!" he confirmed, laughing even more, now at the scowl on her face.

"Tyler!" she shouted before punching his arm softly and laughing with him.

"Come here," he said, holding his arm out. She moved closer and snuggled up to him.

She inhaled the familiar scent of his aftershave and smiled to herself. She was back exactly where she belonged; with him.

"You really waited for me." She spoke softly as she played with one of the strings of his hoodie.

"I told you I would, didn't I?" he replied.

"You did, but didn't you meet anyone?" she asked, feeling guilty that he put his life on hold just for her.

He shook his head. "I didn't feel the need to. I wasn't interested in other girls and besides, how could I have dated someone else when I was still madly in love with you," he declared and her heart melted.

He was the cutest person ever. He held her close and cherished the moment he had been waiting for.

That evening, Tyler took her to his small but cozy one-bedroom apartment. She had said that she would stay in a hotel until she figured something out but he insisted that she stayed with him. She pulled on an oversized sweatshirt that matched her sweatpants and tied her hair up into a messy bun before joining Tyler in the kitchen. He was busy cooking their dinner and it smelt delicious. He was so different from Brad and it was so refreshing for her.

"Do you need a hand?" Holly asked as she stood next to him and watched him cook.

"Nah, I've got this. You make yourself at home. Do you need anything?" he asked, turning his attention to her as she jumped up onto the kitchen counter. She shook her head and continued to watch him.

They enjoyed the rest of their evening together and enjoyed each other's company. She felt so happy with him and just so complete. Her face was hurting from laughing so much and she loved it. It was so nice for her to not be crying for once.

"Oh, Hol, I put your stuff in my bedroom. You can sleep there and I'll crash here," he said, after he took his eyes off of the T.V. and noticed her yawning.

"Uh, are you sure?" She asked as she rubbed her eyes.

"Yeah. If you need anything then just come through and get me, OK?" he said.

"OK. I think I'm gonna go to sleep now. Goodnight Ty," she mumbled, the tiredness clear in her voice. She walked over to him and gave his shoulder a squeeze.

"Night babe," he replied, flashing her a soft smile.

***

She tossed and she turned and she just couldn't sleep despite being so tired. She put a pillow over her face and she could have screamed because she was so frustrated. She smiled happily when she realised that the pillow smelt like Tyler. She wondered if he was still awake or if he was sleeping so she decided to go and check. She tip-toed from the bedroom to the living room, trying her best to be as quiet as possible, in case he was sleeping. The T.V. was still on, at a really low volume and he clutched the remote in his hand. He lay on the sofa in a pair of black basketball shorts and a plain black hoodie. She tilted her head and peered round the hood of his hoodie that he had up.

"Woah!" Tyler shouted when he noticed Holly standing in front of him.

"I'm sorry! I didn't mean to scare you," she laughed, putting one hand over her mouth to try and control her laughter.

"Are you OK?" he asked sweetly, looking up at her.

"Can't sleep," she said and slightly pouted her bottom lip.

"Me neither," he gave her half a smile.

She picked up his legs and collapsed onto the sofa, putting his legs on top of hers. "Sorry, I'll get up," he said, starting to move to let her have more space.

She placed her hand on his leg. "It's fine." She went quiet for a moment and he continued to watch T.V.

"Can I ask you something?" she blurted before beginning to bite her nails.

"Sure." He turned the T.V. off so that she had his undivided attention and waited for her to continue.

"You know that day I left?" she asked to which he pulled a face. "When you told me you loved me, or even today when you said you were in love with me, did you mean it?" she quizzed him.

"Yeah. I still love you," he clarified, reaching out and holding her hand.

"I love you too. You still wanna give this a go?"

"Yeah. Only if that's what you want as well. I don't want to pressurise you into anything."

"Are you sure? Am I really what you want?" she asked with a sad look on her face.

He sat up when he noticed the look on her face. "Look, I think you're amazing and you're beautiful and you're smart. I love all of your little habits, like biting your nails when you're nervous. I love everything about you. So yeah, I'm sure." He comforted her and gave her a look of reassurance.

"I'm sorry. It's just because he made me feel like I was never good enough for him. Maybe I deserved that though."

"He obviously didn't see you properly or know you the way that I do otherwise he would have loved you, appreciated you and never would have taken you for granted. What he did to you was abuse; both physical and verbal. It's not acceptable at all and I'm glad he is paying for it now. No one should ever have to go through what you went through. Just because he was a hotshot lawyer who felt like he was superior never gave him the right to abuse you and make you feel so worthless. He's just a monster and I don't want you to ever feel like you deserved any of that."

"You know, I gave him everything. And all he did was just take, take, take until I had nothing left to give," she said before sighing and looking into space.

He saw the pained expression on her face and it made him mad as he thought about everything that Brad had put her through. She was a giver, that was for sure. A giver of love, of second chances, of a lot of things. Perhaps that was her downfall at times. Maybe she gave too much and, in the end, maybe that's why it hurt so much when she didn't get anything back.

"Come lie with me," he spoke softly as he lay back down and made space for her. "If you want to, obviously."

She lay with him, his arms wrapped around her. She put her head on his chest and she could feel his heart beating.

"Thank you," she said softly. "For everything."

"You don't have to thank me." A moment of silence passed between them before he continued, "You know, he was a jerk and I'll never, ever, ever treat you the way he did. OK?" He said quietly, finally beginning to feel sleepy.

"OK," she repeated, her eyes feeling heavy.

He held her close, gently massaged her head and ran his fingers through her hair until she fell asleep before falling asleep himself.

Chapter Sixteen

She woke up the next morning in Tyler's arms, feeling so content. Things were looking good and she wanted to enjoy every little bit of happiness that she got. The police had been in touch with her earlier that morning and had reassured her that the situation with Brad had been dealt with and that she wouldn't be seeing or hearing from him for a while. She instantly felt so relieved when she heard the news and was really looking forward to putting everything behind her. She was looking forward to moving on with her life that had been controlled for so long. She looked over at Tyler who was still sound asleep, his messy hair sticking up in so many places. She smiled at the sight of him and felt a sense of contentment. She gently ruffled his hair before climbing off of the sofa to start her morning.

Half an hour later, Tyler joined her in the kitchen to help make the breakfast. He smiled when he saw her, busy cooking and doing her thing. He felt so lucky and thankful that she had made it back to him. He walked over to where she was standing and gave her a big bear hug from behind, resting his chin on her head.

"Good morning!" Holly chirped and greeted him with a huge grin.

"Morning, Hol. You sleep OK?" he replied as he took a few plates and glasses out from the cupboard.

"Yeah, did you? I'm sorry if I kept you up with all my chatting."

"Don't be silly. It's good to talk about stuff. You need to let it all out and I'll always be here to listen. Oh and yeah, that was one of the best sleeps I've had in a while," he said as he set the table.

She put the pancakes onto the plates and put some Nutella over them before adding some strawberries. It was Tyler's favourite breakfast so she thought that she would make it for him. It was the least he deserved after everything he had done for her but it was a start.

"Wow, pancakes! How did you —?" he said as they both took a seat at the table.

"Good memory." She cut him off and smirked slightly to which he laughed. "You told me once so I thought I'd make you some."

"Thank you! This is weird isn't it? Having breakfast together," he asked before he began eating.

"I thought it was just me! It's nice though. It's definitely something I could get used to," she admitted.

"Me and you both. OK, don't kill me but you have about an hour to get ready before we need to leave."

"What? Where are we going?" she questioned before taking a sip of her juice.

"Uh, the airport," Tyler blurted, a smile forming on his lips.

"Erm, why? Are we going on holiday?"

"Not quite. We just have somewhere to be and that's all I can say just now. You'll find out the rest when we get there."

"Oh my god! I'm excited! Confused but excited."

He laughed. "Don't be confused. Just be excited and trust me!"

She beamed as she finished off her food, her mind full of thoughts about where they could be going.

"Hey Hol?"

"Yeah?"

"Don't ever let that smile fade," he spoke softly as he admired her pretty smile.

***

After four hours and forty-seven minutes, they arrived at their destination. Tyler had done a good job so far at not letting slip about why they were going away. He just had to keep it up for another five minutes. He climbed out of the cab and got their luggage before helping Holly out. He had managed to keep her blindfolded once they got out of the airport as he didn't want her to find out anything else. She had figured out that they were going to New York City when they got into LAX and saw the flight schedules but he didn't want her to know anything more.

"Tyler! I don't like this. Can I please just take this off now?" Holly pleaded as she clung onto Tyler, terrified in case she fell.

"Babe, just two minutes. We're almost there. I just need you to climb the stairs OK?" Tyler replied and guided her up the stairs.

"OK, just don't let me fall."

"I've got you, Hol."

He led her up the stairs and got the driver to help him take up the luggage. They took the elevator up to the eighth floor and he guided her towards the door, the driver following behind. Tyler reached for the keys in his jacket pocket and opened the door.

"You can leave that there. Thank you so much," Tyler said to the driver who put their luggage inside before smiling and taking off.

"OK, you ready?" Tyler asked, taking a quick look around to make sure that nothing was out of place.

"I'm ready, I'm ready!" Holly squealed, she could hardly contain her excitement.

He slowly took off her blindfold and stood next to her, anxiously watching as she took in her surroundings.

"Welcome to your new apartment, Hol," Tyler said softly with a warm smile on his face.

"OH MY GOD! Are you joking? This is insane!" she exclaimed as she looked around in awe.

"I'll show you the best bit, come here." He gestured and led her to the living room window.

She gasped as she saw the spectacular view of Central Park. "Tyler! This is crazy." She flung her arms around him and he admired the happiness that practically radiated from her. It was all he wanted. "Is this really my place?" she continued. She was in a state of slight shock.

"It is. I promised myself that if you ever came back to me, I would do whatever it took to get you to New York City and make your dreams come true," he revealed as they stood side by side admiring the view.

"That's the cutest thing ever. Thank you so much! I love you!" she said, giving him another hug.

"It's OK. Make yourself at home. I'm just going to go and pick up some food from across the street. Will you be OK?"

"Yeah," she said as she began to wander around.

He was such a sweet person. He had actually remembered everything she had told him about how she envisioned her dream apartment. It was up high, it was a two bedroom, it was cosy and the colours were perfect. She came across a room that had the door firmly closed and she contemplated whether or not to go in as she didn't want to be nosy. Her curiosity took over and she remembered that he did say to her to make herself at home. She opened the door and gasped at once when she realised what it was. It was the spare room she spoke about that contained a bookcase against the wall with some of her favourite books there. He had even got the colours right and she was really amazed. It was black and white and it was perfect. There was a swivel chair and desk against the other wall and as she admired the little things laid out on the desk, she noticed a letter that was addressed to her. She took a seat and began to read. She recognised his handwriting straight way and couldn't help but smile. The letter read:

Holly,

If you're reading this, it means that you are finally free and we found each other again. I've been waiting for this day for a very long time and I am so glad that it is finally here and you're safe. I hope you like your new place and I hope I got everything right. Take a look around, this is your space, your room, your place. It's all yours. You deserve all of this. You have been through so much and you deserve all of the happiness in the world. I want you to know that I have a lot of time and a lot of love for you. You are so special to me and I knew you would be the second I laid eyes on you. You're an incredible person with such a big heart. You are so beautiful and you have the best smile that makes me a little weak inside. I hope this makes you smile and I hope you know how amazing you really are. Don't ever change for anyone. Enjoy this new chapter of your life. I hope it's everything you've always dreamed of.

Love you,
Ty. x

Just as she finished reading, the buzzer went and she quickly wiped her tears and went to answer the door. Tyler stood opposite her with food in one hand and a bunch of flowers in the other. He flashed her a smile and she leaped into his arms, almost knocking the stuff out of his hands but she didn't care. She just loved him so much. He put down what he was holding and gave her a tight squeeze before spinning around with her in his arms. They both laughed before he put her down.

"What was that for?" he asked as they both made their way to the living room to have their dinner.

"I just have so much love for you, Ty," she gushed before sitting cross-legged on the floor, her back leaning against the sofa.

"I would hope so," he joked, his slim frame leaning against the door of the living room.

He stood in silence as he looked at her and looked around, taking a few minutes to take it all in. She noticed the silence between them and looked up to find Tyler admiring her, half a smile on his face.

"Don't look at me like that!" she said as she blushed before smiling herself.

"Why not, huh?" he replied and walked over before taking a seat next to her. She rolled her eyes at him, still smiling. She was so happy that she just couldn't stop smiling.

"So, tell me, how long have you been planning this?" Holly asked, a curious look forming on her face.

He put one arm around her and reached for a slice of pizza with his other hand before replying. "Honestly? The day you left. I started planning it all and then it was just back and forth from here and there. I stayed here quite a bit but don't worry, I never made any mess!" He laughed as she leaned into him.

"I think this is the sweetest thing anyone has ever done for me," she said as she lightly caressed his face, his beard prickling her fingers a little.

"It's what you deserve after everything you have been through."

She smiled sweetly at him. "Oh by the way, this isn't my place. It's ours," she said.

"Really? Are you sure? I didn't know how you would feel about me and about everything so I was just thinking when I was planning everything, that I would get my own place somewhere."

"Don't be silly. I want you to stay with me!" she spoke. She squished his cheeks before continuing, "I want to wake up to this face every day." She laughed and he kissed the palm of her hand.

"I promise you that everything will be OK from now on and that I will never stop trying to make you happy," he promised. She winced at the sound of the word 'promise'. "What's that face for?"

"Oh, I've just got a thing with promises. They always get broken so I'm not a fan of them," she sighed.

"Well lucky for you, I don't make promises that I can't keep. So just forget about all the previous promises and all of that stuff, OK?"

He rubbed her back as if to comfort her and she realised that he was right. She had to forget about everything that had happened and leave it in the past where it belonged.

"Here's to fresh starts," Tyler said, raising his glass.

"Fresh starts," she repeated as their glasses clinked.

She was so ready to start afresh. She was excited for the first time in ages about what the future held for her. She gazed at him lovingly for a few seconds. It was the most perfect little bubble that they were living in and she wanted to live in it forever.